# BLINKY

Blinky and his Dad Frost visited Snowfalls Island when Blinky was born. Blinky was born with magic eyes that require magic drops to control the outcome of his magic. The drops were to be found on the Island. During the visit to the Island there was a Blizzard where Blinky and his Dad became separated. Frost couldn't find Blinky and had to return home without the baby. He could no longer find peace without his Son, so Frost decided to revisit the Island every year in hopes of his return. It is very important for him to find Blinky. I know We got separated and now he is alone and scared not knowing how to control the outcome of the magic he was born with. I must not give up until I find him.

Blinky blinks his eyes and a Snowman by the name of Patch appears. Blinky asked are you my Dad? He replies no I'm sorry my name is Patch. I don't know how I appeared so suddenly. I'm sorry says Blinky that may be my fault. I blink and things appear out of my control. I'm trying to find my Dad Frost he will know how to fix it. We were separated a few years ago and I've been searching for him forever.

While stumbling along Blinky blinks, trips and falls over a branch rolls down a hill and loses his head. Another Snowman appears and asked how did I get here? My name is Brooms do I know you? I'm sorry says Blinky it's all my fault. I blinked and you appeared. Can you help me pickup my head and place it back on my body? I lost it during the fall.

Blinky blinks again and another Snowman appears. Hello! my name is Cracker not sure how I got here but it's nice and cold outside. Would you like some peanut butter and crackers? No thanks, says Blinky just looking for my Dad. Well don't give up the Winter has just begun, and you may find him yet.

How did you guys get your names? They call me Patch to help those in need. A patch goes a long way to help cover the hurt. They call me Brooms because of the broom. This broom has enough magic to take you all around this Island. They call me Cracker because of the peanut butter and crackers but my magic is in my smoke pipe.

Do you think my Dad will find me Patch? Of course, he will keep your head on kid. I would look for a kid like you forever. You are on a Magical Island where magic is just around the corner. Hang in there Blinky.

Blinky there is a Snowman on the other side of the Island that has magical eye drops says Patch.

Magic Drops

Half of cup of Snow

Half of cup of Ice

Half of cup of Rainwater

Mix together and apply to blink

Cures most magical uncontrollable outburst

Mr. Snowman can I have some magic drops? Well ok I'm saving some for my Son when I find him. We were separated a few years back and I've been searching for so long. I really miss him. Sir is your name Frost? Yes! it is do you know me? It's me Dad Blinky. I have been searching for you for a long time and now here you are. Blinky I'm so glad that you found me. I been searching for a long time too Son. I have your magic drops Son. Let's fix it and go home.

The End

1

Blinky was born with Magic eyes.

Magic with Uncontrollable Outburst.

Snowfalls Island

Frost and Blinky

The Blizzard that separated Blinky from his Dad.

5

Blinky blinks and Patch appears.

How did I get here?

I appeared suddenly!

Do you think my Dad will find me Patch?

Of course he will, keep your head on kid.

 I would look for a kid like You forever.

You're on a Magic Island.

Hang in there Blinky!

Blinky blinks, trips and falls and loses His head.

Will You help me pickup my head and place it back on my body?

I lost it during the fall.

7

This Broom has enough Magic to take You anywhere on this Island.

8

Hello my name is Cracker.

I'm not sure how I got here.

It's nice and cold outside.

How did you guys get your names?

They call me Patch to help those in need.

A little patch can go a long way to cover the hurt.

They call me Brooms because of the broom.

This broom has enough magic to take you all around this Island.

They call me Cracker because of Peanut butter and crackers.

My Magic is in my smokepipe.

Patch

Broom

12

Smoke Pipe

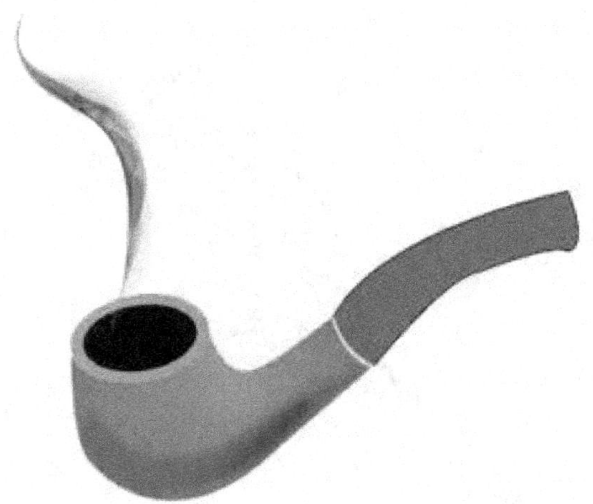

Peanut butter and Crackers

14

Frost searching for Blinky.

I know He's scared.

I left Him all alone.

Oh Blinky I'm so Happy that You found Me!

I have the Magic drops.

Let's go Home Son.

16

I'm going Home.

I found my Dad!

BLINKY

17

Magic Drops

18

Magic Drops

Half of cup of Snow

Half of cup of Ice

Half of cup of Rainwater

Mix together apply to Blink

Cures most Magical Uncontrollable Outburst

I LOVE
WINTER

The End

ISBN 9798612046271
90000
9 798612 046271

CHARLES RIVER EDITORS
HANDSOME LAKE